THE STAR CHILDREN

Written & Illustrated by Jill Yasmin Kaplan

Awakening Press

Published by
Awakening Press
998 61 st Street Oakland, CA 94608
www.SattvicHealing.com

First Edition

Written & Illustrated by Jill Yasmin Kaplan
Book design by Norman Clayton, Ojai, California

Library of Congress Control Number: 2011907899
Kaplan, Jill Yasmin / The Star Children

ISBN-13: 978-1463711986

DEDICATION

I offer my deepest gratitude to David and Elaia for their steadfast support and love.
Thank you Chase, Reed, and children everywhere, for being such great lights.
My heartfelt thanks to Gurumayi and the Siddhas for their ever present grace.

May we all shine!

The star children played in glittering
meadows. They delighted in the beauty all around.

Some raced and skipped about while others
gathered bouquets of flowers.

They frolicked in glorious gardens filled with wonderful colors and fragrances, and swam in streams of sparkling waters where winged creatures bathed.

A group of children sat down
and closed their eyes.

They could see the earth,
far in the distance.

There were majestic purple mountains,

vast oceans with sandy beaches,

flat golden plains, green rolling hillsides,

and long stretches of parched land.

They saw people planting orchards of delicious fruits and berries. Their gardens were bursting with flowers and vegetables. They tended each plant, stone, and creature, with great care. Father sun shone his golden rays. Brother wind spread seed. Sister rain gave pure waters to thirsty plants, and the light of the stars and moon shone upon them.

Continuing to gaze, they saw other people at work.

Many moved quickly from one place to the next.

They looked tired and hungry.

They didn't rise in the morning wondering what

marvelous things they'd see or do.

"Ah," said one of the star children, "Some of the people have forgotten their light." One by one others spoke...

"I want to help the earth children. I'll sing for them."

"I'll tell them stories to help them remember their light."

"I'll encourage everyone to believe in themselves."

"I will teach them to grow gardens that nourish everyone."

"I'll race with them in meadows and remind them to play."

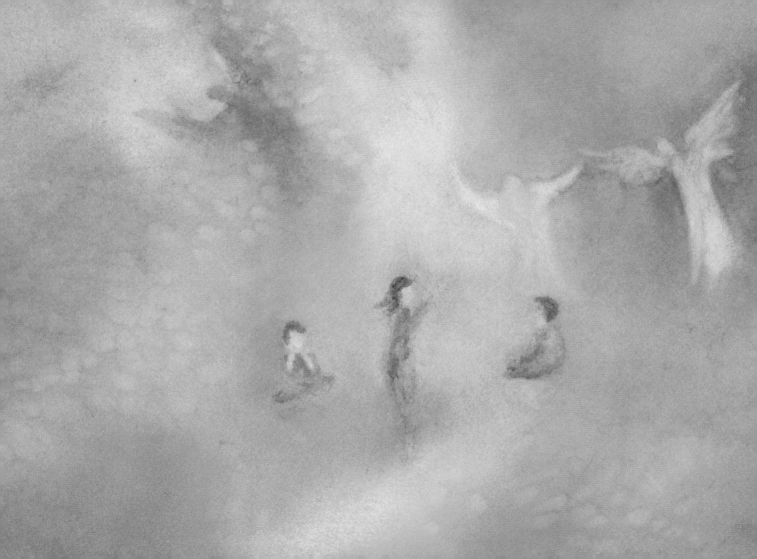

One by one, the star children shared their resolve to go
to the earth to share their light, love, and wisdom.
Angels appeared and said, "Your return to earth is glad news.
You will help many."

"It is not easy though to stay awake. Earth's gravity is strong.
Some people on earth are awake. We will all help you. Remember
to go inside to your heart. There we will connect in love."

The star children were led down the rainbow bridge to earth
to the mothers and fathers who awaited them joyfully.

Of course when they arrived they were little babies.

The light of love shone all around them and within them

and they grew and grew.

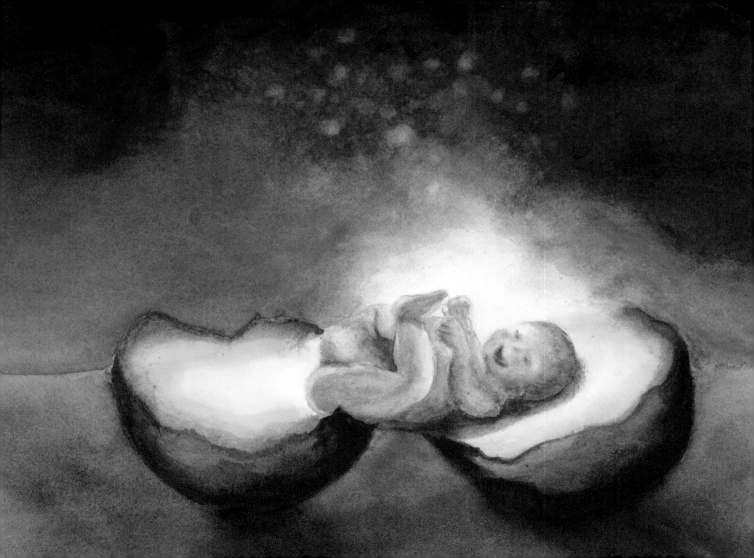

At last the day came when they went off to school.

Their teacher told stories of the star children. They sang...

"The sun is waking. Night's falling away. Rise and shine, it's a brand new day. The sun has risen the day is new. Let's open our eyes. What will we do?"

A gentle breeze carried the message from afar...

Remember... who you are.

What will you do?

Made in the USA
Charleston, SC
25 February 2012